Usborne Farmyard Tales

TRAIN STORIES

Heather Amery

Illustrated by Stephen Cartwright

Edited by Jenny Tyler

Language Consultant: Betty Root

There is a little yellow duck to find on every page.

Notes for Parents

Train Stories is a collection of four delightful stories from the *Farmyard Tales* series of picture books. Your child will want to share it with you many times.

All the *Farmyard Tales* stories have been written in a special way to ensure that young children succeed in their first efforts to read.

To help with that success, first read the whole story aloud and talk about the pictures. Then encourage your child to read the short, simpler text at the top of each page and read the longer text at the bottom of the page yourself. Taking turns with reading builds up confidence and children do love joining in. It is a great day when they discover that they can read a whole book for themselves.

The *Farmyard Tales* series provides an enjoyable opportunity for parents and children to share the excitement of learning to read.

Betty Root

THE OLD STEAM TRAIN

This is Apple Tree Farm.

This is Mrs. Boot, the farmer. She has two children, called Poppy and Sam, and a dog called Rusty.

“Hurry up,” says Mrs. Boot.

“Where are we going today?” asks Poppy.
“To the old station,” says Mrs. Boot.

They walk down the lane.

“Why are we going? There aren’t any trains,” says Sam. “Just you wait and see,” says Mrs. Boot.

"What's everyone doing?" asks Poppy.

"They're cleaning up the old station," says Mrs. Boot. "Everyone's helping today."

"Poppy and Sam can help me," says the painter.
"Coats off and down to work," says Mrs. Boot.

Poppy and Sam work hard.

Sam brings pots of paint and Poppy brings the brushes. Mrs. Boot sweeps the platform.

"What's that noise?"

"It's the train. It's coming," says Mrs. Boot. "Look, it's a steam train," says Poppy. "How exciting."

The train puffs down the track.

It stops at the platform. The engine gives a long whistle. Everyone cheers and waves.

“Look, there’s Dad,” says Sam.

“He’s helping the train driver, just for today,” says Mrs. Boot. “Isn’t he lucky?” says Poppy.

"All aboard," says Mrs. Boot.

"I'll get on here," says Poppy. "Come on, Rusty," says Sam. "I'll shut the door," says Mrs. Boot.

“Where are you going?”

“Aren’t you coming with us?” asks Sam. “You stay on the train,” says Mrs. Boot. “I’ll be back soon.”

"Look, there she is."

"She's wearing a cap," says Poppy. "Yes, I'm the guard just for today," says Mrs. Boot.

Mrs. Boot waves a flag.

The train whistles and starts to puff away. Mrs. Boot jumps on the train and shuts the door.

"We're off," says Sam.

The train chugs slowly down the track. "Doesn't the old station look good now?" says Poppy.

"I like steam trains," says Sam.

"The station is open again," says Mrs. Boot. "And we can ride on the steam train every weekend."

RUSTY'S TRAIN RIDE

This is Apple Tree Farm.

This is Mrs. Boot, the farmer. She has two children, called Poppy and Sam, and a dog called Rusty.

They are having breakfast.

“What are we doing today?” says Sam. “Let’s go and see the old steam train,” says Mrs. Boot.

“Come on, Rusty,” says Sam.

They walk down the road to the station. “Don’t let Rusty go. Hold him tight,” says Mrs. Boot.

They wait on the platform.

Mrs. Boot, Poppy and Sam watch the train come in. Mrs. Hill and her puppy watch with them.

The train is ready to go.

Everyone talks to the train driver. The fireman shuts the doors. He climbs on the train.

“Where’s my puppy?”

“Mopp was with me on the platform,” says Mrs. Hill. “Now he’s gone.” The train starts to move.

Rusty watches it go.

He pulls and pulls and runs away. Then he jumps through an open carriage window.

"Come back, Rusty," shouts Sam.

Rusty looks out of the window. "There he is," says Poppy. "He's going for a train ride on his own."

"Stop, stop the train," shouts Sam.

Mrs. Boot, Poppy and Sam shout and wave.
But the train puffs away down the track.

“What shall we do?”

“Both dogs have gone,” says Sam. “We’ll have to wait for the train to come back,” says Mrs. Boot.

At last, the train comes back.

"Look, there's Rusty," says Sam. "You naughty dog, where have you been?" says Poppy.

The train stops at the station.

The fireman climbs down from the engine. He opens the carriage door.

“Come on, Rusty.”

“Your ride on the train is over,” says Mrs. Boot. Rusty jumps down. “What’s he got?” says Sam.

"It's my little Mopp."

Mrs. Hill picks up her puppy. "Poor little thing. Did you go on the train all by yourself?"

"Rusty went with him," says Sam.

"That's why he jumped on the train," says Poppy.
"Clever Rusty," says Sam.

WOOLLY STOPS THE TRAIN

This is Apple Tree Farm.

This is Mrs. Boot, the farmer. She has two children called Poppy and Sam, and a dog called Rusty.

This is Ted.

He drives the tractor and helps Mrs. Boot on the farm. He waves and shouts to Mrs. Boot.

“What’s the matter, Ted?” asks Mrs. Boot.

“The train is in trouble. I think it’s stuck. I can hear it whistling and whistling,” says Ted.

“We’ll go and look.”

“Poppy and Sam can come too,” says Mrs. Boot. “And Rusty,” says Sam. They walk across the fields.

Soon they come to the train track.

They can just see the old steam train. It has stopped but is still puffing and whistling.

“Look at those sheep.”

“They are on the track,” says Poppy. “That’s why the train has stopped.” “Silly sheep,” says Sam.

“It’s that naughty Woolly.”

“She’s escaped from her field again,” says Poppy.
“She wanted to see the steam train,” says Sam.

“We must move them.”

“You can help me,” says Mrs. Boot. “Come on, Rusty,” says Sam. They walk up to the sheep.

"How can we get them home?"

"We can't get them up the bank," says Ted.
"We'll put them on the train," says Mrs. Boot.

"Come on, Woolly."

They drive the sheep down the track to the train. Woolly runs away but Rusty chases her back.

“We’ll lift them up.”

“Please help me, Ted,” says Mrs. Boot. Ted and Mrs. Boot lift the sheep up into the carriage.

"All aboard!"

Poppy, Sam, Mrs. Boot, Ted and Rusty climb up into the carriage. Mrs. Boot waves to the driver.

The train puffs along.

It stops at the station. Mrs. Boot opens the door. Poppy and Sam jump down onto the platform.

"How many passengers?" says the guard.

"Six sheep, one dog and four people," says Mrs. Boot. "That's all."

"Let's all go home now," says Mrs. Boot.

They take the sheep back to the farm. "I think Woolly just wanted a ride on the train," says Sam.

DOLLY & THE TRAIN

This is Apple Tree Farm.

This is Mrs. Boot, the farmer. She has two children called Poppy and Sam, and a dog called Rusty.

Today there is a school outing.

Mrs. Boot, Poppy and Sam walk down the road to the old station. “Come on, Rusty,” says Sam.

“There’s your teacher,” says Mrs. Boot.

“And there’s the old steam train, all ready for our outing,” says Poppy.

“All aboard,” says the driver.

The children and their teacher climb on the train.
The guard closes the door and blows his whistle.

Mrs. Boot waves goodbye.

The train puffs slowly down the track. Rusty barks at it. He wants to go on the outing too.

The children look out of the window.

“I can see Farmer Dray’s farm,” says Sam. “Why has the train stopped?” asks Poppy.

"The engine has broken down."

"We'll have to send for help," says the driver. "It won't be long." The guard runs across the fields.

"Here's a ladder."

"You can all get off now," says the driver. "We can have our picnic here," says the teacher.

"Let's go into the field," says Sam.

The children climb over the fence. "Stop! Come back, children," says the teacher. "There's a bull."

"It's only Buttercup."

"She's not a bull. She's a very nice cow," says Poppy. "Well, come back here," says the teacher.

“Look, there’s Farmer Dray.”

“He’s brought Dolly with him,” says Sam. “A horse is no good. We need an engine,” says the teacher.

The children watch.

Farmer Dray has a long rope. He leads Dolly along the train. The driver unhitches the engine.

The children climb back on the train.

“We’ll soon be off now,” says the teacher. “Dolly’s ready,” says Farmer Dray.

"Pull away, Dolly."

Dolly pulls and pulls. Very slowly the train starts to move. Farmer Dray walks along with Dolly.

They reach the station.

“Out by engine, back by horse,” says Farmer Dray
“That was a good outing,” says Sam.

First published in 1999 by Usborne Publishing Ltd., Usborne House, 83-85 Saffron Hill, London EC1N 8RT, England. www.usborne.com

Printed in Belgium. First published in America in 2000. UE.

Wood yard
Ted's house
The donkey shed
Camping field
The cow field
(a balloon landed here once)
The barn
Scarecrow field
Apple Tree Brook
This line is for goods trains.
Woolly the sheep
This is where Woolly the sheep stopped the train.
Old mill
Castle ruins
←To Market Town